Baby Be Mine:

Lovin' on My Block Boy

Nikki Rae

Baby Be Mine: Lovin' on My Block Boy

Copyright © 2020 by Nikki Rae

Published by Tyanna Presents

www.tyannapresents1@gmail.com

This is a work of fiction. Any references or similarities to actual events, real people, living or dead, or to real locals are intended to give the novel a sense of reality. Any similarity in other names, characters, places, and incidents are entirely coincidental.

§*Synopsis*§

Marrying the love of her life, Delante is one of the things Ka'Myra feels like she got right in life, besides her kids. But all of that changes when Delante's career starts to interfere with their marriage, and Ka'Myra feels the distance etched in all of his late nights at work. Will her husband's carelessness about her feelings cause Ka'Myra to jump into the arms of another man?

Let's find out in this dramatic rollercoaster ride in "Baby Be Mine."

Is Delante and Ka'Myra's love story a classic? Or are they so blinded by love, they can't see it's a fairytale approaching it's ending?

§*Chapter One*§

Ka'Myra

"**B**itch, I know damn well you can see that he's wearing a wedding ring, so I suggest you get your thirsty ass up out of his face before you have a big problem on your hands," I snapped on the chick that was invading my husband's personal space. I did random pop ups on Delante. I didn't play about mine. "As a matter of fact, take a break. My husband will let you know when to return."

Delante rubbed his hands down his face and shook his head. Once the room was empty, Delante finally said something.

"Yo', you really need to chill with this bullshit. You're fucking with my money and making it uncomfortable for my clients," Delante said with an attitude.

"Delante, I don't give a damn about those thirsty bitches feelings. If they're here to make music, then that's what they need to be doing instead of being up in your face. And you be with the shits 'cause every time I walk in, your ass be in here showing all thirty-two's like you at a fucking dentist appointment. I told you, Delante. I don't play when it comes to mine," I sassed.

"Ka'Myra, how many times do I have to tell you that I'm not worried about those bitches, I gave you my last name for a reason. If I still wanted to play in the streets, then I wouldn't have married you. I don't know what happened to the sweet, innocent, shy girl I married. Your ass is batshit crazy now, damn. I know I be laying down some great dick, but chill, ma. It's your dick; I ain't going nowhere," Delante stated. I just rolled my eyes at his dumb ass.

"Look, I just don't like seeing those women in your face, and when you don't put them in their place, they're gonna think they have shot. Which is gonna cause them to get their ass kicked. But I have a few errands to run, so I'm gonna go. You know Valentine's day is in four weeks, and this big ass vow renewal we're throwing is taking a lot of work, but it will pay off in the end."

"Yeah well, those errands are gonna have to wait. Since you made me miss out on money, take you fucking clothes off. You owe me an hour worth of pussy," Delante stated seriously. Delante went to go lock the door and pull down the shades.

"Delante, I have to go," I whined.

"Okay, you can go in an hour when I'm done busting that pussy open," Delante said while stripping me out of my clothes.

I didn't even bother to fight him because I knew he wouldn't let me leave until he got what he wanted. My husband and I fucked all of the studio for a little over an hour. Once we were done, we decided to go get some lunch. I was still in love with my husband after being married for five years. Delante was my everything and I was his. I wasn't used to being jealous but Delante made me crazy and couldn't picture my life without him.

During lunch, Delante helped me with some of the shit that needed to be done for the party.

Valentine's Day was four weeks away, and we were throwing a big Valentine's Day party. We decided to renew our vows that same day. It was a lot of work, but I knew in the end, we would have a great time. It would be well worth it. I had to meet Tyisha at the mall, and I didn't have to worry about rushing because Delante was picking up the twins. Plus, our live-in cook was gonna make dinner tonight. Some nights I still cooked dinner for my own family.

I pulled up at the mall and Tyisha was sitting in her car on the phone. Once she saw me, she ended her call and got off the phone.

"Hey, bestie. You looking good," Tyisha greeted.

"You looking pretty good yourself. Why the hell you got me at this mall around Valentine's day? This shit is packed as hell," I stated.

"Girl, just bring your ass on. I need you to help me get something for a Calvin," Tyisha replied.

We shopped and walked the mall like we owned it. We watched the hating ass bitches stare us down and roll their eyes, but we just giggled. Tyisha and I had most definitely upgraded from the project chicks that we used to be. We both owned our own businesses and had men with their own businesses and money. But no matter how much money we had, we'll never forget where we came from. I felt someone staring a hole in my back, and when I looked back, it was a group of young girls staring, but the pregnant one stuck out for some reason. I wasn't sure who she was, but she was staring at me like she knew who I was.

"Damn bestie, why the hell is that young girl starring at you so damn hard?" Tyisha asked. At first, I thought I was tripping, but now that I knew I wasn't. The young girl really had my mind going. I was used to women staring, but my gut told me this was personal.

"Girl, I don't know, but I was just thinking the same thing before you said anything. As long as her little ass don't say shit to me, then she's good because I don't have a problem with smacking a bitch," I told Tyisha, and she chuckled at my comment as we walked into Macy's. This was the last store before going home. I needed to grab some smell goods for me and Delante. After paying for my items, we walked out the store, and the same group of girls that were staring at me was now standing outside of Macy's.

"Um, do y'all little girls have some kind of problem?" Tyisha asked with attitude, beating me to the damn question.

"No, ma'am. We're sorry for staring, but my friend Brittany was scared to come over and talk to Mrs. Green," the girl stated.

Now I really wanted to know what the hell was going because it was clear that she knew who I was. I just wished I knew who the hell she was and what she wanted.

"Listen, I really don't have all day, so can you say what you need to say so I can leave this damn mall," I stated, feeling agitated.

"I'm pregnant by your son Amir," the pregnant girl blurted, and my heart damn near stopped because I knew I didn't hear her correctly.

"I don't know what type of games y'all little girls are playing, but I'm not in a playing mood."

"Mrs. Green, I wouldn't dare play around about something like this. I just turned four months yesterday. My parents just found out last week, and they're pissed off. They plan to come to your house some time this week. Amir and I were messing around for a couple of months until I told him I was pregnant, and now he barely answers my calls. I don't know how he could do this to me. The only time I see him now is if I pop up at his set or wait for him to finish basketball practice," the girl Brittney informed me.

"What do you mean pop up on his set? And are you sure that this is my son's baby?"

"Yes, I'm sure this is Amir's baby. He's the only person I've ever been with, and Amir sells weed. I'm not trying to start any trouble. I just don't want to be as a single mom at this age, I'm already scared, and I'm hurt that he's treating me like this. Amir said that he loves me, but I can't tell." I couldn't believe what the fuck I was hearing.

I was gonna fuck Amir up and why the fuck would he be selling weed? I thought.

"I'm sorry for my son's behavior. Listen, I have to get home, but I would like to give you my number to give to your parents so we can sit and talk this out and I would like to have theirs as well. I'll handle Amir, but whatever you do, don't tell him about our conversation."

"Thank you, and I don't think he would talk to me long enough for me to tell him anything," Brittany said sadly.

Hearing her speak like that about my son had me in my feelings because I raised him better than that. After we exchanged numbers, me and Tyisha headed out the mall.

"Damn Ka 'Myra what the hell are you going to do?"

"Before or after I fuck him up? Look, let me get going I have some shit to deal with," I told Tyisha before getting in my car.

The conversation that I had with Brittany kept playing over and over again. I decided to call Brittany's parents to see if the three of them was available to come over for dinner tonight because I needed to get to the bottom of this shit. I called the number and the phone rang three times before someone finally answered.

"Hi, my name is Ka'MyraKa'Myra Green. Your daughter Brittany gave me your number. She told me that she's pregnant by my son and I would like for the three of you to come over to dinner so we can talk. I just found out a few minutes ago, and I'm not happy with what I heard."

"Hi, my name is Kimberly, and me and my husband and Brittney will be there. Just send me the time and address, and thanks for reaching out," Kim replied.

After ending our call, I called Tyisha and asked her to pick up Kamil and Kamar because I didn't want them at the house. My next call was to Brian. I didn't tell him what was going just that I needed him at the house at seven.

****

Later that evening, the house was a little awkward because I had yet to share with everyone what was going on, but I was walking around tight-faced. I was disappointed in my son, especially since he knew what I went through as a young single mom. That's one of the main reasons I think it had so much effect on me. Brian had done the same shit to me, and now my son thinks he will walk in his father's footsteps? Amir had the game fucked up if he thought that was gonna happened. Then to hear he sells drugs really burnt a hole in my heart.

"Baby, what's going on? What's this meeting about?" Delante asked.

"Everyone will find out soon enough," I replied. The doorbell rang, and I knew it had to be them since Brian was already there.

"I'll get the door," I said as I walked to let my possible extended family in.

When we walked into the dining room, Amir spit his drink out and his eyes widened so damn big that they looked like they were gonna pop out of his head. Brittany's father face was probably just as tight as my face was.

"Everyone, this young lady here is Brittany, and these are her parents. She tells me that she's carrying Amir's baby," I blurted. The room was silent, and I could tell that everyone was shocked by what I said.

"Amir, do you care to fucking explain this?" I asked angrily.

"Mom, I'm sorry. I swear I was gonna tell you," Amir replied.

"When were you gonna tell me, Amir? She's four months pregnant, so when exactly did you plan to say something? Not only that, but Britany also said you've bailed on her and keep avoiding her calls since she's told you that she was pregnant. Is that true?" I yelled.

"Baby, calm down. Let's just talk about this. Hi, I'm Delante. I'm Amir's stepfather, and this is his father, Brian, and Amir's twin sister Amira. Please sit down."

"Amir, is this your baby?" I asked, getting straight to the point.

"Yes, I believe so. I took her virginity," Amir admitted.

"So, why the fuck would you neglect her and stop talking to her knowing that's the same thing your father did to me? Do you know how hard it was raising a set of twins as a teenager, and you gonna do the same thing? I am so fucking disappointed in you that I can't even look at you right now. I raised you better than this Amir."

"I'm Brock, Brittany's father. My wife and I just found out our daughter was pregnant last week. My first thought was to go off the deep end, and I would have if my daughter would have told who the boy was. Obviously, it takes two to make a baby, but my baby girl is only fourteen years old. I'm not happy, and she's too far along to get rid of the baby. She has her entire life ahead of her, and now, she's gonna have a fucking baby. What do you plan to do about this?" Brock asked Amir.

"He's gonna man up and take care of this child. We can assure you that. I don't know what has gotten into him, but he will be there every step of the way. Your daughter will no longer have to do this alone," Delante assured Brittney and her family.

I was too pissed to say anything right now. Moments later, we were finally eating dinner. We continued to talk about future plans and doctor's visits. Once dinner was over, our company left and I still had one more thing to address. I walked up to Amir and without warning, I punched him in his chest with every bit of strength in my body and knocked the wind out of his ass.

"So, you're a fucking drug dealer now? I don't know what the fuck you doing with your life, but this shits stops right the fuck now! I'm over you, Amir!" I yelled before storming off, leaving my family standing there.

§*Chapter Two*§

Delante

It's been a little over a week since we found out that Amir had a baby on the way and was selling weed. Ka'MyraKa'Myra was still pissed to the max and was in rare form just about every damn day. I think the situation triggered her childhood memories and everything that she went through. I've been talking to Amir daily, and he's been doing much better. He damn sure ain't slinging weed no more. My wife shut that shit down and embarrassed his ass in the process, so I know he won't call himself selling shit again. Planning this vow renewal on top of everything that's been going on was becoming stressful, and I couldn't wait until this shit was over.

I just pulled up to one of my artist's house to go over this new contract. When I got there, shorty was wearing this skimpy ass nightie. I couldn't lie; shorty was thick as hell, but I knew it would be a bad idea to go into that house. I had never cheated on my wife before, but this shit was tempting. I was still a man.

"Look, I know that this is your house, but I'm a married man, and I'm uncomfortable coming in with you wearing that. I'm your boss, so please go put some clothes on," I stated.

"Oh, you're one of those men who only can reject a sexy woman if she's fully dressed, huh? Well, like you stated, this is my house, and this is what I would like to wear. If you can't keep your hands to yourself, that's on you," she stated. I knew I should have just left, but against my better judgment, I went in. Qiana sashayed into the living room, and that ass was looking good.

"Here's the contract for you to sign," I told her, handing Qiana the paperwork. She seductively signed, then sat it back on the table, walking closer to me.

Once she was invading my personal space, Qiana dropped to her knees, freed my manhood and started sucking the shit out of my dick. I threw my head against the wall and enjoyed the soul snatching that was taking place by Qiana's mouth. I felt my dick pulsating in her mouth and I knew I was about to cum. I tried to pull her mouth away but she kept going, swallowing my seeds. After catching my breath, I quickly came to my senses and snapped out.

"Why the fuck would you do some stupid shit like that? I told you I was a married fucking man! I don't think I can work with you. This was a mistake!" I yelled while fixing myself so I could get the fuck out of there.

"Oh, trust me, we'll be working together. I'm sure of that," she replied with a sneaky smile. It was something about the way she said that shit that didn't sit well with me, but I flew out the door feeling like shit. I didn't think I would be able to keep this from Ka 'Myra. As soon as I got in the car, I called the one and only person I knew I could talk to. I knew that he would keep my secret.

"Yo'! Wassup, bro?" Calvin answered on the first ring.

"Yo', where you at? I need to holla at you; I need someone to talk to."

"Yo', you good? Where you wanna meet? I'm on my way."

"Meet me at our spot," was all I said before hanging up. I knew he would know where I was talking about because we've been going there since we were kids.

Ten minutes later, I pulled up to Charlie's bar in Camden. I needed a drink bad as hell. Not long after I got there, Calvin walked in.

"Yo' wassup? This shit sounds important."

"I fucked up big time. I went to take a new client her contract, and she answered the door in some nightie. I knew I should have left, but being stupid, I went in. After she signed the paper, she started sucking my dick. Yo', that shit had the nerve to be super fucking good. I told her I didn't think I'll be able to work with her and she said but you will. It was something about the way she said that shit didn't sit right with me," I explained.

"Damn. Well, just keep it business, and I pray to god Ka'Myra doesn't find out," Calvin stated.

"Nah, I think I need I need to tell Ka'Myra. We don't keep secrets," I said to Calvin.

"Look, you need to take that shit to your grave. It's not like you fucked her. If you tell her that crazy shit, her ass is gonna leave your ass but do what you feel is best."

I just listened to Calvin as he talked, but I didn't expect to get the best relationship advice from him because he still fucked around on Tyisha from time to time. I told him that shit wasn't cool. Because once you make someone your woman or your wife, that fucking different bitches had to stop. And the last I checked,

Calvin was a married man but that didn't stop him if a bitch caught his eye.

An hour later, I finally took my ass home. When I pulled Ka'Myra wasn't home yet, and I was kinda glad because I could get in the bathroom and wash that bitch Qiana off my dick without Ka'Myra becoming suspicious. Once I was finished with my shower, I walked into my office and ordered my wife some roses. I really felt like shit about today. We only had two weeks to go before for the big day, and I wasn't trying to fuck that up.

Me: Hey, baby. Just wanted you to know that I was thinking about you. I love you more than you'll ever know.

My pride and joy: I love you too, baby. Is everything okay?

Everything in me wanted to tell her what happened but I just couldn't bring myself to do it.

Me: Yeah, babe. Everything is great. I'll see you when you get home.

I paged our cook Vanessa to tell her to make a separate meal for me and Ka'Myra and told her that we'll be needing a candlelight setting in a private room setup. It was time to pick up the twins, and as I was getting in my car, I could have sworn I saw Qiana pulling off. But I knew I had to be tripping because why the hell would she be around my way. As soon as I walked into the twins' school, the receptionist eye-fucked me like she always does when I pick the kids up, but I didn't even smile at her like I usually I do.

"Daddy!" My baby girl yelled while jumping in my arms. I kissed her cheek and hugged her tightly.

"Hey, dad. Wassup?" Kamar asked like he was grown. My kids were something else.

"Wassup, son?" I had to go pick up Amir and Amira from school because ever since my wife found out about what Amir was up to, he had no free time. I thought she was being a little hard, but you can't tell woman shit when it comes to their kids. After picking up the kids, we headed home.

When I got in., Ka 'Myra was already in the house in the shower. I waited for her in our bedroom with my pants off and dick in hand. I needed to feel my wife before and after dinner. When Ka 'Myra walked out in the room, she just smiled and headed towards me.

Ka 'Myra climbed on top of me and kissed my lips while putting the tip of my dick into her opening. That's the one thing I could say about my wife; she always knew what time it was without me saying anything. My wife was a freak, just liked I liked my woman. After a few minutes of her bouncing her sexy ass on my dick and moaning in my ear, I came hard and fast, and so did she. After I cleaned my wife up then myself, we headed downstairs so we could help the twins with their homework and have dinner.

§*Chapter Three*§

Ka'Myra

This week has been super busy. It was four weeks before the wedding, I still had so much to do, and the shit was becoming stressful. Especially with everything that has been going on in the home front. Amir was making me a grandmother at an early age, on top of thinking he was gonna sell drugs. Amira wanted to date, and my husband has been acting super strange.

For the past week, Delante has been super nice and catering to my every need. Not to mention sending flowers damn near everyday, which is why I was surprised that it was now noon and I have yet to hear from him. Being super nice and romantic, but I could feel in the pit of my stomach that something was wrong. I just didn't know what. Most people would call me crazy for complaining about my husband.

I called him three times but he didn't answer. I planned to pop up on his ass after I left my hair shop over Philly. I opened two shops, one in Camden on Market Street and the other over in Philly. Business was great and I still had a few clients hair that I still did regularly but for the most part, I just ran the shop. After stopping pass both of my shops, I decided to pop up on my husband. When I got to the record label, I went straight to Delante's office but he wasn't there so I took it upon myself to turn on the camera's and see where he was. When I finally located him, I thought my eyes were playing tricks on me because there was no way in hell that my husband was getting his dick sucked but a woman other than me.

I felt like my soul was just crushed, and my heart was beating fast, but instantly all that hurt turned into anger. I flew out of the office, never even bothering to turn the cameras off. I rushed down to studio three, damn near kicked the door off the hinges, and grabbed that bitch by her hair.

"You can't see that this is a married fucking man!" I yelled while crashing my fist into the girl's jaw. Delante was yelling out something, but he knew not to put his hands on me. "You sucked the wrong married dick," I yelled again, this time hitting her even harder.

"Get the fuck out of here and never show your fucking face here again or I'll kill your ass the next time," I spat. The girl was scrambling to get her things together so she could leave. I turned my attention to Delante.

"How could you do this to me to our family?" I yelled, swinging on Delante like he was stranger in the street. He was trying to block my hits but wasn't successful. "I fucking hate you, Delante!" I yelled.

"Ka'Myra, I'm sorry. Please let me explain; it's not what you think," Delante said, pissing me off even more.

Men say the dumbest shit. How is it not what it looked like when I clearly watched another woman sucking my husband's dick? The bitch had the nerve to be good at it.

"Fuck you, Delante, and fuck this marriage. I suggest that you find yourself a hotel to stay at, but I'm done with your cheating ass!" I yelled while throwing my wedding ring at him.

I was hurt beyond words. I didn't even realize that we had an audience until I turned to walk out. Delante called out for me, but I ignored him and kept walking until I reached my car. Once I got in the car, I cried and banged on the steering wheel. I couldn't believe that Delante was cheating on me. I had all kinds of thoughts running through my head. Like how long and why?

I wasn't ready to go home yet, and I needed somewhere to go, so I went to Tyisha's boutique because I really needed to talk. Twenty minutes later, I pulled up to Tyisha's clothing boutique. When I walked in, I didn't see her in the front so I headed to her office. I didn't even bother to knock I just walked in.

"I'm sorry just to barge in, but I really need to talk to you," I cried. Tyisha jumped up from her desk and walked over to me.

"Oh my god! Ka'Myra, what's wrong? Why are you crying?" I couldn't even get the words out at first. I just cried for the first few minutes before finally speaking.

"I just caught Delante cheating on me. I didn't hear from him all day, so I went by there after I left the shop, and some bitch was sucking his dick in one of the studios. I beat the shit out of her and him. How could he do this to me?"

"I am so sorry. I'm so shocked that I'm speechless," Tyisha stated while hugging me tightly as I cried and getting snot all over her shirt.

"I'm done with him, Ty. I can't stay with him after what he did. I gave him his ring back and told him to find somewhere else to stay because I'm through with his ass," I told her honestly.

"Ka'Myra, I know you're hurting right now, but don't you think you should think about this before you throw five years of marriage down the drain over a dick suck?" I looked at Tyisha liked she had three heads because I knew she wasn't suggesting that I sweep that shit under the rug.

"I know you're not suggesting that I sweep this shit under the rug and act like it never happened?"

"That's not what I'm asking you to do at all. But I am asking that you think about this before you throw away your marriage. The both of you vowed for better or worse that's all I'm saying," Tyisha stated.

"Well, that's not gonna happened. He should have thought about those same vows before he threw away our marriage over a dick suck. I just hoped it was worth it. I'm out, it's clear that I came to the wrong place. I thought I was talking to my best friend and not a damn marriage counselor," I threw over my shoulder while walking out the door. I knew deep down Tyisha was only trying to help, but I didn't need that right now.

* * * * * * *

Later on that evening, I was taking a long soak in the jacuzzi sipping on my second glass of wine. After feeding the kids, helping with homework, and making sure Amir and Amira were good. I locked myself in the room, crying into my pillow so no one could see or hear me. Delante and Tyisha were both blowing up my phone to the point I just turned my phone off because I didn't want to deal with anyone. Once I was finished soaking, I climbed out the jacuzzi, dried off, and walked into my bedroom but instantly become enraged when I saw Delante cheating ass on sitting on the bed.

"Delante, why the fuck are you here?" I yelled.

"Ka'Myra, I know you're pissed, hurt, and I'm sorry for being the reason you're in so much pain, but I never meant to hurt you. I swear I didn't. But what I won't do is lose my wife of five years over the first fuck-up that meant nothing. And I'm definitely not getting no hotel room. I will go to sleep here and wake up here as long as we have children, so you can get that out of your mind. Now I will sleep in another room, but I'm not leaving the house."

"Fuck you, Delante. I hate you and can't stand to look at you right now." Delante just stood there sadly as if he could feel my pain.

"Baby, I'm sorry, but please just let me explain, so there will be no secrets. I should have told you the first time because you deserve to know the truth." Hearing Delante say, "the first time" caused my heart to drop because it sounded like he was insinuating that this has happened before.

"What do you mean the first time?" I asked, trembling scared to hear his answer.

"Look, baby, I fucked up. Last week when I made my rounds to drop off contracts, the bitch that you saw at the studio literally just started sucking my dick. I tried to stop her at first, but after a while, that shit started feeling good, so I let her finish. As soon as she was done, I cursed her ass out. I told her that I couldn't work with her, but she didn't seem bothered. Come to find out, she planned the entire thing and recorded it so she could blackmail me. I found out yesterday. She told me the only way you wouldn't see the video is if I let her suck my dick again and give her twenty thousand dollars. I was stupid and fell for the shit, thinking it was over. I didn't really plan to give her the money once she gave me the tape. My first thought was to kill that bitch, but I figured this way was easier. I'm really sorry. I put that on everything," Delante pleaded.

I wasn't sure if I was more hurt or more shocked about the shit that Delante just said, but all I could do was cry. I felt so betrayed by him, and I didn't want anything to do with him again. At least that's what I told myself. I looked at Delante with so much pain and anger in my eyes. I couldn't speak because I didn't have the words to say.

"Can you please go find somewhere to sleep? I can't bear to be around you for a second longer," was all I that I could come up with. Delante looked like he had something he wanted to say, but the death stare I gave him let him know to save the bullshit. Once he walked out the room, I locked the door behind him, climbed into bed, and cried myself to sleep.

§*Chapter Four*§

Tyisha

The past couple of days has been crazy. Ka'Myra still wasn't fucking with me, and Delante was in my ear about still moving forward with the wedding, but the way shit was going, I didn't see that happening right now. Even if she did decide to stay with his ass. I was lying in bed watching Calvin sleep after our hour-long fuck session. I put the pussy on him so good he didn't have a choice but to go to sleep. The only reason why I was still woke is because I had a lot of shit on my mind. Ka 'Myra not talking to me was really fucking with me, and after I picked up my son Cameron from school, I was gonna go pay her stubborn ass a visit because the shit wasn't cool. Ka 'Myra and I had never stopped speaking before, so it was killing me. The sound of Calvin's phone vibrating broke me from my thoughts, but Calvin didn't even budge. As soon as the phone stopped, it dinged, indicating that he had a text message. So, my nosey ass decided to read it, but I made sure that I left it on unread.

*Unknown: **Damn, daddy, I thought you were coming through? We miss you.***

I wanted to reply so fucking bad. Calvin really had me fucked up if he thought he was just gonna do him while I sit around playing house with his ass. I was hurt and my heart was beating fast. I wanted to beat him out of his sleep, but I talked myself out of it. The nerves in my stomach were doing backflips, and it felt like I had to vomit. I jumped up and ran into the bathroom because I really did have to throw up. I swear it felt like I was kneeling at the toilet forever.

"Babe, you good?" I heard Calvin's voice say. It took everything in me not to jump up and punch him in his face, but I needed to play my part.

"Yeah, I'm good," I said, getting up from the toilet to rinse my mouth out. Calvin turned the shower water on. I instantly grew suspicious since we agreed to stay in the house and lay up all day until it was time for me to pick Cameron up from school.

"Why you getting in the shower? I figured we'd go a few more rounds, then I'll make us something to eat."

"As good as that sounds, I'm gonna have to take a rain check. Something came up at the shop, so I have to handle that shit. Trust me, bae, I'm just as pissed as you are. But I promise I'll make it up to you as soon as I get home tonight," Calvin stated, lying through his teeth. I knew that Calvin was lying; I felt it in my gut. Calvin hopped in the shower, so I rushed in the room and grabbed his phone. After what I read, a part of me wish I didn't.

Me: Baby, I'll be there soon to see you and my baby girl, but don't text back my wife is home today. I told you about texting me when I'm home.

My heart was literally in my stomach. I quickly put a locator on his phone, so I could see what the fuck he was up to. The one thing I knew was there was another woman in the picture. I prayed baby girl was a nickname for her pussy and not a child because I would lose my shit, kill his ass, and probably her too. I was for sure that I was gonna need my best friend after reading the shit that I just read. I couldn't believe he would do this to me then he climbed out of bed and reneged on our plans for that bitch. Hurt was an understatement. I ran to the bathroom and threw up again. This time I wasn't at the toilet as long as the first time.

"Yo', your ass in here throwing up again? Are you sure that you good, baby?"

"I'm just fine," I stated sarcastically. I was pissed, but it's not like I could tell him I'm throwing up because I know he's cheating on me, and it literally made me sick.

"Yo', wassup up with the attitude?" That cheating bastard had the nerve to ask.

"I'm just upset that our plans got interrupted, and you have to leave. You do realize that I took off from work to spend time with you, and now you're bailing on me?" I lied, rolling my eyes.

"Baby, I'm sorry. I swear I'll make it up to you. I know that you and Ka 'Myra ain't talking, but maybe you can get Amira to keep Cameron for us. We'll spend the entire day and night together just the two of us, but for now, I have to go. But here, take this and go shopping; buy whatever you want and pick up something sexy for tonight and tomorrow." I just took the card and hugged Calvin. I knew that we weren't gonna have a special night tonight or tomorrow if what I suspected about him was true. I'll probably need a sitter until I got out of jail, which I would use his card to post bail.

As soon as Calvin left, I took a shower then put on some black tights, a shirt, and a pair of sneakers. I needed to be comfortable. I put my hair in a ponytail, making sure not to leave anything hanging. I put on a pair of studs because I still needed to be cute in case I did have a run-in with his mistress. I didn't want to look busted and disgusted.

When I was ready to go, I pulled up his whereabouts, and just as I thought, his ass wasn't at work. But when I was through with his ass, he was gonna wish that he did take his ass to work. Calvin and I have been married for three years now. We didn't have anything big, but we did have a small destination wedding in the Bahamas. It was small yet beautiful, and a day I'll never forget. I took my vows seriously, but apparently, Calvin didn't take them as serious as I did. I grabbed my belongings and headed to Cherry Hill, which is where the tracker said he was at. Fifteen minutes later, I pulled up to the address, and sure enough, my husband's car was parked in the driveway. Before getting out, I had to get my feelings intact. I didn't have time to be overly emotional at this time. I walked up and knocked on the door hard enough for the neighbors to hear, but no one came to the door, so I knocked again.

"Who is it?" I heard a woman's voice ask.

"You have a flower delivery," I lied. The woman opened the door with a smile on her face and skimpy ass robe on, but her smile quickly faded when she was met with my fist. But I didn't stop there. I barged in, rushing her to the floor, and she let out a loud scream. "Where the fuck is my husband?" I yelled, hitting her again, but my question was quickly answered when I heard Calvin's voice.

"Nikki, what the hell is going on?" Calvin asked but quickly stopped in his tracks when he realized what was going. I looked up, and my heart dropped when I noticed that he was holding a beautiful baby girl. The baby looked like she was about six months or so.

"Oh fuck! Baby, I'm sorry! Fuck!" Calvin yelled while placing the little girl in her playpen. I totally lost it at the moment and starting throwing wild hits on the woman that mothered a child with my husband. Calvin was grabbing at me, and once he was able to get me off the woman, I turned my anger to him, which was the person I should have fucked up first anyway. I started swinging wildly on Calvin and landed a few good hits until he finally overpowered me. "Tyisha, chill out! I'm sorry, just let me explain."

"Calvin, get your crazy ass wife out of my house!" The woman yelled.

"Don't worry, bitch, I'm leaving, but not until I'm ready. Is that your fucking baby, Calvin?" I yelled. The baby was crying, and my emotions got the best of me. Now I was standing in this woman's living room crying.

"Come on, baby. Let's go. Let me explain," Calvin pleaded.

"Fuck you, Calvin. How could you do this to me? You had a baby with this trick ass bitch? You fucked around on the wrong bitch, Calvin, and you most definitely fucked the wrong woman's husband," I said calmly before walking out the door.

"I'm gonna have you arrested for assaulting me," that dumb bitch yelled.

"Do what the fuck you gotta do!" I yelled back.

I wasn't sure why I was suddenly so calm. I think my hurt took over my anger. I couldn't believe that Calvin had a baby with another woman outside of me. Seeing him holding the little girl did something to me that I don't think I'll ever get past. I made it to my car, and Calvin was on my heel, but I got in my car and peeled off. I didn't know where else to go, so I decided to try my luck with my best friend. I pulled to Ka 'Myra's house in ten minutes and was happy to see her car in the driveway. I got, rang the bell, and Ka 'Myra answered the door in her pj's.

"Tyisha, what happened? What's wrong?" No words would come out. All I could do was cry hysterically.

"Tyisha, talk to me. What's wrong? Did somebody die?"

"He has a baby, Ka 'Myra. He really has a fucking baby," I repeated.

"Tyisha, calm down. What are you talking about? Who has a baby?"

"Cavin has a baby! I can't believe he would do something like this to me. Cheating is one thing, but a baby is another thing. How could he do this to me?" I cried.

"Omg! I'm so sorry, Tyisha. I swear I am. I can't even imagine how you feel right now," Ka 'Myra stated, hugging me tightly. My stomach started turning, and I jumped up to try to make it to a trash can, but I didn't make it. I ended up vomiting all over Ka 'Myra's floor.

Once I was finished throwing up, I cleaned up my mess. And Ka 'Myra went to get me something to drink. We sat at the table and I told her everything that took place today. I could tell that my story hit a soft spot for her. Now I understand how she was feeling when she came to me that day, and now, I felt like an ass.

"I wish I had the words to say to take this pain away, but I don't. What I can do is be a listening ear and a shoulder to cry on."

"Bestie, I'm sorry I wasn't a better support when you came to me about Delante. I missed you so much and wondered how things were going with you and Delante."

"It's cool, we're back now, and I'll catch you up about us later. Right now, fuck both of them cheating ass niggas."

****

Someone banging on my door woke me up from sleep. I looked over at my phone, and it was six in the evening, and I wasn't the type of person that had company over. I jumped up and answered the door, still wiping the cold out of my eyes. I opened the door to find two police officers at my door.

"Are you Tyisha Jenkins?" The lady officer asked.

"Yes. What's this about?"

"Ms. Jenkins, you are under arrest for the assault against Miss Nakita Young. You have the right to remain silent. Anything you say can and will be used against you in the court of law. You have the right to an attorney. If you cannot afford one, will be appointed for you.

"Can I at least put my shoes and coat on? And are the cuffs really necessary?"

"Yes, I can take you to get your shoes and coat, but the cuffs are necessary. As long as you act like you have some sense, I won't put them on tight," the officer answered. I wasn't surprised that bitch would have me arrested. I bet she thinks she's gonna one day live happily ever after with my husband, but I had news for her dumb ass. That shit would never happen as long as I had blood flowing through my veins.

§*Chapter Five*§

Calvin

I was sitting in Charlie's bar getting plastered all by myself. That shit that happened earlier today with my wife and my daughter's mother had my head fucked up. I had every intention on telling her about the baby. I just didn't know how. Nikki don't even mean shit to me; I just fucked up and got her pregnant. I mean, we do fuck here and there, but I ain't been off that shit with her. Lately, when I go over there, I'm with my daughter. I tried calling her a million times, but she wouldn't answer. But I couldn't blame her for that. Nobody knew about the baby, not even my best friend. But I knew at this point he had to know because he's been blowing my phone up. Nikki has been calling and texting since I left her house, but the only person I wanted to talk to was Tyisha.

"Yo', I've been calling your ass all day long to see what the hell was going on. Why the hell you didn't you answer any of my calls?" Delante asked while taking a seat on the empty barstool next to mine.

"I just didn't want to be bothered. I'm fucked up right now and need some alone time," I slurred.

"Nigga, that shit ain't gonna happen. You need to go get your wife out of jail?" I knew I was drunk because I thought I heard Delante say Tyisha was in jail.

"What the fuck are you talking about? Why the fuck would my wife be in jail?" I asked, sobering up really quick.

"Why don't you ask this baby mom of yours that I'm just hearing about?" I knew what he just said, but I pulled out my phone and dialed Tyisha's number. The voicemail came straight on, so I called Nikki because I know damn well she didn't have my wife locked up.

"Hello," Nikki answered with an attitude.

"Yo', did you have my fucking wife arrested?" I yelled through the phone.

"Did you really think I was gonna let her get away with coming to my house and putting her hands on me?" She got the game fucked up.

"Do you know how bad you just fucked up? you gonna regret that shit. You ain't nothing but a fucking bitch ass for doing that. Don't ever call my fucking phone again, bitch!" I yelled before hanging up. I rushed out the bar with Delante n my hip.

"I'll drive," Delante said. We hopped in Delante's car and peeled off. About ten minutes later, we was pulling up in front of the county. The car had barely come to a complete stop before I hopped out. When I walked into the county, the first person I saw was my mother in law and Ka 'Myra.

Before I could get a word out of my mouth, my mother in law slapped the shit out of me. I swear if she wasn't my wife's mother, I would have stretched that bitch out right there in the county.

"How fucking dare you cheat on my daughter and get some tramp pregnant? And because she beat the shit out of your hoe ass baby mama, she gets locked up? That bitch deserved whatever ass-whooping Tyisha put her on ass and some. Hell, you need your ass kicked too. Why the fuck are you even here?" My mother in-law screamed.

"Look, with all due respect, Ms. Wilson, this is between me and my wife," I told her.

"The hell if it is and you mean soon to be ex-wife. I'm gonna make sure my daughter has the best damn divorce attorney there is to have and take your black ass for everything. Now don't contact my daughter again," my mother in-law stated seriously. For some reason, her words cut deep and pissed me off.

"You really need to mind your damn business. That's my wife and you can save that divorce attorney for someone else because my wife and I aren't getting a divorce. Now, I'll admit that I fucked up and I'm gonna do everything in my power to fix my mess, but that's between me and my wife," I told my mother in-law seriously.

"And one more thing, please don't ever put your hands on me again," I warned.

"Why the fuck are you here, Calvin?" I don't have a damn thing to say to you, and please let your bitch now that this is just the beginning. I'm ready to go. I really need to shower and wash this place off me, Tyisha stated before walking off leaving me standing there like I was a nobody. I tried calling after her, but she didn't even look back.

"Yo, just give her some time, man. This shit is a lot to take in. She's hurt, pissed, and I'm sure she's embarrassed. But whoever this baby mom of yours is, needs to be put in her place," Delante said.

I knew he was right, but for tonight I just wanted to go sleep and hope when I wake up, all of this shit was a dream.

Delante dropped me off at home and as soon as I got in the house, I went upstairs, stripped out of my clothes, climbed into my bed, and drifted off to sleep. I knew Tyisha wasn't coming here tonight and my son was at Ka'MyraKa'Myra's so he was straight.

* * * * *

It's been three days and Tyisha sill wouldn't even talk to me. I decided to stay at a hotel to avoid any bullshit. Plus, I didn't want my son to see me and his momma beefing. As far as Nikki and I haven't talked to her ass either. She's been calling and texting every day, but I had to cool down before speaking to her before I did something I would regret. I just walked into my mom's house, and the vanilla candle scent was smelling good throughout the house. I found my mom in the kitchen cleaning collard greens.

"Hey, mom. Wassup?" I greeted her with a kiss on the cheek.

"Hey, son. Wassup? I hear you fucked up pretty bad this time," my momma said, shaking her head.

"Yeah, I take it that you talked to my wife? I don't know what the hell I was thinking, mom. Then Nikki getting her arrested didn't make the situation any better. Tyisha won't return any of my phone calls. I love that woman with everything in me and it took me not talking to her for a few days for me to realize that I can't live without her. I just don't know how to fix this, but what I do know is I'm gonna fight for my marriage until I have no fight left in me."

"Well, son, that's what marriage is, it's work, and you have a lot of work to do. You hurt that poor girl to the core. Hell, I'm just as pissed and disappointed at your simple ass as she is. The problem with y'all niggas is y'all only know how to think with y'all dick and not your brains. Even if she decides to work it out, you have to be patient and wait on her to be ready. Y'all men fuck us over and hurt us, then tell us how long we can be upset or hurt about it. Shit don't work that way. And I don't mean to sound rude, but I'm not claiming this so-called daughter of yours until you get her tested. Don't trust these skanks 'cause we both know these hoes ain't loyal."

I just shook my head at my mom 'cause she be saying some crazy shit out of her mouth. but I knew she was only speaking the truth.

"Yeah I know, mom. Anyway, let me get going. I have some shit that I need to handle and a marriage to save. I love you, mom," I told her before heading out. The first stop I was making was Nikki's house. It was time for me to put some shit in order.

When I got to the house, I didn't even bother to knock. I used my key in walked in. When I got to the top of the steps, I thought I was tripping because I could have sworn, I heard moaning coming from Nikki's bedroom. Before I opened the door, I went to find my daughter; she was sleeping peacefully in her room. I walked over to her crib and gently kissed Kalie on her forehead before exiting the room to see her trifling ass mother. I opened the door, and some skinny ass nigga was balls deep in Nikki. I stood there for a few seconds before making my presence known. Now I felt where my mom was coming from about getting the blood test because, honestly, until now, I never thought for a second that Kalie wasn't my daughter.

"So, this is what we do now, Nikki?"

"Oh my god!" Nikki yelled, trying to push the nigga off of her.

"Yo, who the fuck is this?" The dude asked.

"Apparently, I'm a fucking fool, but listen up, Nikki. I'm not gonna hold y'all up, but please understand that whatever we had going on is done and over with. I'm working shit out with my wife. And as far as Kalie, I want a DNA test immediately. If she turns out to be my daughter, then I'll take care of her, but I'll set up arrangements to pick her up. Also, my wife says this shit is far from over. Y'all enjoy the rest of y'all day, you hoe ass trick," I threw over my shoulder as I was leaving. I could hear the two of them having words, but I didn't give a fuck about any of that.

When I got back to my car, I just sat there thinking about what the fuck just took place. I didn't so much care about her fucking another nigga because I was a married man, but all I could think about was how my marriage could be over and Kalie may not even by my daughter.

Kalie was six months, and I haven't missed a moment of her life. I made sure she was straight and made sure to see her at least three times a week, so she'll know who I was. I would be a little heartbroken if she turned out not to be mine, but for now, I would have to wait it out. I was on my way home to see if I could win back my wife. I knew it wouldn't be easy because Tyisha was a tough cookie to break. She wasn't the one to take no shit. When I pulled up, I was happy to see Tyisha's car parked outside. I stuck my key in the door, and Cameron jumped off the floor.

"Daddy, where was you?" Cameron asked, jumping up in my arms. I knew I couldn't lie to my son, so I told him the truth without all the adult details.

"Son, daddy did something wrong that mommy wasn't too happy about, so I had to give mommy some space and time to calm down. I needed some time to think about what I had done and how could I fix it. When you do something wrong or hurt someone's feelings, you have to do more than say sorry. You have to show them that you won't hurt them again."

"Okay, so what are you gonna do for mommy? Are you gonna buy her something nice?" Cameron asked, causing me to snicker. My son was something else.

"I'm gonna have to do more than buy something nice, but that's a good start. As a matter of fact, why don't you go get dressed so you can help me pick out something nice? But stay upstairs and play until I call you down, I need to talk to mommy alone," I told Cameron.

"Yayy!" Cameron yelled, running up the steps.

"Calvin, why are you here? Tyisha asked, breaking me from my thoughts. I looked up at my wife, and although she was in lounge around clothes, she was looking good as hell. I was missing Tyisha like crazy.

"Look, baby, I know that I'm the last person that you want to see right now, and I completely understand, but I need to get a few things off my chest, and I really need you to hear me out. Can you please come sit down so we can talk?" I asked Tyisha. She just stood there for a few seconds without saying a word before making her way to the couch.

"Calvin, make it quick because I have shit to do," Tyisha said with an attitude. I didn't expect anything less.

"Baby, I know I fucked up beyond words. I would never able to take what I did back, but I love you and my son with every fiber in my body, and I couldn't imagine my life without y'all. I'm sorry you had to find out the way you do, but what I need you to know is I never meant for this shit to happen. I only fucked her twice. I know that don't change anything, but I swear she don't mean shit to me, Tyisha-" she cut me off by but her hand up.

"Please don't do that, Calvin. How the fuck you gonna sit here and tell me that she didn't mean shit? I just caught you playing house with that bitch, and now she don't mean shit? Are you finished because this conversation isn't helping you at all?" Tyisha snapped.

"Look, you're right. What I'm trying to say is I can't lose you, Tyisha. I'm begging you not to leave me. Everything will be on your terms. We can take it as slow as you want, and you can be as mad and hurt as you need to be. I just don't want to lose you. I swear you're the air that I breathe. I thought I was a tough guy that didn't need a woman until I met you," I pleaded. I didn't even realize that I was crying until I felt a tear roll down my face. Tyisha was just looking at me with tears in her eyes, but she didn't say anything. I tried my luck and reached for her hand, and surprisingly, she let me.

"Please, baby, say something. Let me get a sitter for Cameron, and we can start with dinner. I'll tell you whatever you want to know," I promised. I couldn't believe that I was begging a woman to stay in my life. Hell, before I started fucking with Tyisha, all I did was fuck bitches and keep it moving.

"Calvin, I don't know what's going to happen with us down the line, but as of today, I'm not ready to go there with you. I miss you like crazy because you mean everything to me. But I can't fuck with you like that. And as far as us going to dinner, I'm gonna have to decline. You didn't just cheat on me; you made a fucking baby on me. And asking me to stay in this marriage is asking me to help you raise and take care of you and your mistress child.

You're also asking me to explain to our son how he has a little sister, but I'm not her mom. You're asking me to pay for your mistake, and that's not fair to our son," Tyisha said as the tears freely fell from her face. I felt like shit and less than a man. I let my family down in the worse way.

"I guess I have no choice but to respect that, but please know I'll never stop trying. I won't give up on you, and that's a promise," I told her seriously. I called Cameron downstairs so we could go to some stores and find some great gifts to get some brownie points.

§*Chapter Six*§

Amir

I couldn't believe that at the age of sixteen, I was sitting in at a damn doctor's appointment with my soon to be baby mom instead of class. I fucked up in the worst way. I was just having fun, I wasn't trying to be nobody's baby dad. Don't get me wrong; I liked Brittany a lot, but I wasn't trying to play house with her ass. I was a typical teenage boy. All I wanted to do was get my dick wet and have somebody to chill with when I wanted to hang out. But my dumb ass got caught out there. My parents wasn't playing no games with my black ass. They made sure I was at every damn appointment. I understood where my mom was coming from since my dad bailed on her when she was pregnant with me and my twin at a young age. My mother was really disappointed in me and hated that I had let her down. I wasn't sure why I did the shit I did. My momma always made sure that we were straight. Once she started fucking around with Delante, we really didn't want for shit. Brittany was scrolling through her phone until the doctor called us to the back.

Today was the day we found out if we were having a boy or a girl, and I was a little excited. I didn't have any doubts that the baby was mine because Brittany was a good girl. I knew for a fact that she was still a virgin when I hit because it took me damn near two days to get through her tight walls. Hell, she was bleeding, and shit. I was just as freaked out as her ass, but once I got in, we were getting in damn near every day. I felt like a dick head for abandoning her once she told me she was pregnant. My best friend tried to talk to me, but I was being an ass.

"Brittany Jones?" The nurse called. We both got up and walked to the back. Brittney laid back on the table, and I sat next to her in the chair. The doctor didn't waste any time getting started with the ultrasound. He put the thing on her stomach, and the baby immediately popped up on the screen. I was amazed and way more excited than I thought I would be.

"The heartbeat is strong and the baby seems to be measuring accurately. Now for the best part, are you two ready to found out what the sex of the baby is?" The doctor asked. We both nodded our heads with excitement.

"It looks like you're gonna be having a little girl," the doctor told us. For some reason that moment was everything to me. It felt like something deep down inside of me had changed and I wanted to do right by my daughter and her mom. Which was why when we left the doctor's, I planned to make it official with Brittany. My baby girl deserved nothing but the best, and so did her mother. The doctor continued the ultrasound as me and Brittany talked among ourselves about our baby girl.

"I'm not sure they missed this, but it looks like there's two of them in here and they're in the same sac," the doctor stated, breaking our conversation and gaining our full attention.

"Did you say it's two of them? And what do mean when you say they're in the same sac?" Brittany asked damn near jumping off the table. I could see that fear had taken over the excitement that she just held.

"Relax, Miss Jones, but yes, you are having twins. And what I meant when I said they were in the same sac is just a medical term for saying they're identical. Do either of you have twins in your family?" The doctor asked.

"I am a twin, I have a twin sister," I answered still in shock.

"Well, this makes perfect sense then. I just don't know how come no one saw that there's two babies before now. That means we're gonna be a little longer because I need to make sure the second baby is healthy and measuring the same as the first baby," the doctor informed us.

"Are they both girls?" I asked.

"I was trying to see what the sex of the baby was, but the legs are closed," the doctor told us.

When we were finished at the doctor's, I called my stepdad to pick us up. I asked Brittany to come over for a few so we could talk, and she agreed. A few minutes later, my stepdad Delante pulled up blasting music. As soon as we got in the car, he turned the music down.

"So will I be having a grandson or a granddaughter?" he asked with a bright smile.

"Well, one of them is a girl, and we don't know what the other one is yet," I told him. I laughed at how fast his head spent around to look at me.

"Are you telling me that y'all having twins?"

"Yup, that's exactly what I'm telling you. We're just as shocked as you are," I told him.

"Damn, your mother is gonna have a heart attack when she hears this shit. And what do you think your parents are gonna say," Delante asked Brittany.

"I honestly don't know; they may kick me out. My parents are very disappointed in me, and we honestly don't talk much. The minute they found out I was pregnant, everything changed, Brittany stated sadly. The car fell silent, and I began to feel like all of this was my fault. Only if I would have just let her be, but nope, I wanted to feel what pussy felt like. When we got to the house, Brittany and I headed straight to my room so we could talk. As soon as we made it in my room, my phone rang, and it was Delante.

"Hello," I answered on the first ring.

"Yo, if you about to fuck in my house, you better keep that shit down, and you bet not get caught by your mama. I'm barely out the doghouse, and I ain't trying to spend no more time in that bitch." All I could do was laugh and hang up the phone.

"Are you good? You've been pretty quiet since we left the doctor's."

"Well, all of this is a lot to take in. I can't take care of two babies; I barely know what to do with one. I never pictured myself being a single teenage mother. I'm almost certain I'm gonna get kicked out the house when I tell them I'm having two babies," Brittany cried.

"Don't cry, ma. We gonna get through this. I'm not saying it's gonna be easy, but we'll get through it. I know I left you and stopped fucking with you when you first told me about the baby, but I swear that shit won't happen again. We're both gonna raise our kids together as a couple if you let me." She looked up at with a surprised look on her face.

"Are you saying that you want to be with me?"

"Yes. I know that we're young, but we can at least try to do the right thing. I don't want you to think I only wanna be with you because you're pregnant. I'm really feeling you. And if your parents do kick you out, that would be fucked up, but you can stay here with me and my family."

"Boy, you know your momma not gonna let that happen."

"My parents aren't happy about me having a baby at a young age either, but they're very supportive and family-oriented. There is no way my mother will see her grandbabies on the street," I assured Brittany.

****

Later that evening, after sexing Brittany in my parent's home, she finally went home to talk to her parents. My mom had already called to let me know that she was on her way home. Things between me and my mom finally seemed like they were finally getting back to normal because she wasn't fucking with me like that when she found out how I was doing Brittany. And when she heard I was selling weed, she fucked me up and made me take the shit back to the person I brought it from. That was probably the worst day of my life. I was so embarrassed. Not only did she make me give the weed back and tell them I couldn't sell anymore, she also whopped my ass.

Them niggas on the block clowned my black ass so bad that I knew I couldn't show my face in the hood no time soon, if ever again. My face was both fucked up my mom had hands for days. I honestly think she took it personally because she was a single teen mom and didn't have much help.

I decided to go see what my twin was doing since I haven't seen her all day. When I got to her room, I could have sworn I heard sniffles at her door. I knocked on Amira's door, and she didn't say anything, so I took it upon myself to walk in. I needed to know why the hell my sister was crying.

"Yo Mira, what's going on in here? Why are you crying?" I asked. Amira looked up at me, but she still didn't say anything. I sat in the side of the bed and demanded answers. It was like Amira to be crying she was always smiling.

"Amira, tell me what the hell is going on now!" I yelled.

"I'm so fucking stupid," she cried, handing me a piece of paper.

I read over the paper and damn near had a heart attack when I saw the words tested positive for chlamydia and trichomoniasis I had to reread that shit because I just knew this wasn't true. I didn't think she would get caught out there like that. I knew my sister was fucking but she didn't tell me about anybody she was seeing lately. I thought she was chilling but I guess not. For some reason, reading that shit angered me and I wanted to know who the hell she was fucking that was going around burning bitches.

"Yo, who gave you this shit? And who are you fucking!" I yelled.

"Lower your voice before somebody hears you, and I can't tell you who it is," she said, pissing me off. I wasn't no snitch but something didn't feel right. My mind instantly went left and thought the worst.

"Oh my god, did somebody rape you?" I asked. Amira slowly nodded her head no.

"What's going on in here?" I heard my mom's voice say, causing me and Amira to both look up at her.

My mother walked in the room over to the bed and took the paper I was holding out of my hand. She read through the paper then and I could see the fire about to shoot out of her face.

"Amira, what the fuck is this shit that I'm reading? So, now you fucking too? You know what? I'm about sick of both of you already. I tried my fucking best to shield y'all from this type of life, but I did it for nothing. You done went and got some young girl pregnant and your ass sitting here with a burning pussy?" My mom yelled.

"Who the fuck is the boy that you're fucking? So I can tell his parents how dirty his dick is. I'm so disappointed in both of you. I'm going to your school first thing Monday morning."

"He doesn't go to my school," Amira stated. I was really confused now because where the hell did she meet this boy. She don't go anywhere but my dad's and Latrice's house.

"We'll talk about this shit later. I'm too tired for this shit tonight," my mom said before walking out the door.

As soon as my mother left out, Amira put me out too. I ain't even bother to argue with her ass. I had my own shit to deal with.

§*Chapter Seven*§

Ka'Myra

Shit has been pretty crazy in the Green house lately. I was starting to question what the hell did I do so wrong to deserve the shit that has been happening lately. My daughter was walking around with a burning pussy, and my son was about to have a set of twins. As far as me and my husband goes, we still weren't doing the greatest. I may have forgiven him by now if that side bitch that was sucking his dick didn't send me a video of her and Delante's first encounter. Not to mention that bitch pressed charges on me. Him and I may have been in a better place. Delante still wanted the wedding vow renewal to happen, but I still wasn't sure if that was gonna happen or not. I completely stopped planning for it. I told him he could continue to plan if he wanted to, but he wouldn't know if I was going to remarry him until the day of.

If I decided that I wanted to renew my vows then I would walk down the aisle to meet my groom but if not, his ass would be sitting there at the altar looking stupid. I knew I didn't want to be without Delante but I had to make him sweat this shit out. Delante needed to know that I wasn't the one to fuck with. I mean yeah, he still cheated by getting his dicked sucked but he at least he didn't fuck another bitch and have a baby on my ass like Calvin did to Tyisha. I felt so bad for her and what she was going through.

Amira and Amir had just walked in the house, but I didn't say shit to Amira since she refused to tell me who burnt her. The only thing she kept saying was he didn't go to her school, so until she was ready to be honest with me, I wasn't fucking with her like that. I know that I was having sex and got pregnant at a young age, but I also had a different upbringing. Not to mention I was in love with Brian when we were together.

"Hey, mom. You good?" Amir asked.

"Hey, Amir. Yeah, I'm good; about to run a few errands. Do you think you could keep an eye on your brother and sister?"

"Yeah, that's cool. I don't have any plans, but Brittany is supposed to stop by."

"Aight well, let me get going." I gathered my belongings and darted out the door. I had to go meet with the party planner to go over a few things for the party. Although I was sure if I was gonna renew my vows or not just yet, we were still having the party since so much money was already spent on it. I couldn't lie, Delante was making it hard for me not to renew my vows with him. He was doing everything in his power to make sure I was happy at all times.

* * * * * *

Two hours later, I was finally pulling back up at home. While I was driving, Brian called and said he was on his way over because he just got back into town and wanted to see the kids, I wasn't even aware that he was away since Amira was always over there. As soon as I got in the house, Kamil and Kamar rushed me. Both of them was trying to jump up in my arms damn near knocking me over.

"Hey, mommy's loves," I said, scooping both of their heavy asses in my arms damn near breaking my back.

"Hey, mommy. Where were you? We was looking all over for you," Kamil asked.

"I had to take care of some business, but I'm home now. I promise that after dinner we're gonna spend some time together just the three of us okay. But for now, go get washed up and ready for dinner."

"Okay, mommy," Kamar said. I put the twins down and they ran off to get ready for dinner. Moments later, the doorbell rang. I knew it had to Brian. When I opened the door, Brian was standing there looking good as shit along with his best friend, Kyree. Kyree and Brian have been best friends since we were in school, but Kyree moved out the hood right before Brian disappeared on me when he found out I was pregnant. But ironically, they both kinda returned back to the hood around the same time five years ago.

"Hey, baby dad. Hey, Kyree," I spoke while letting them both in.

"Wassup Ka 'Myra? And what I tell you about calling me that shit?" Brain fussed, but I didn't care. I will continue to call him that just because I knew he hated it.

"Anyway, what brings you by here?"

"My kids, of course. I mean, maybe if you weren't married, I would be coming to see you too," Brian flirted as he always did when my husband wasn't around.

"But she is married and will remain a married woman until death do us apart, so stop flirting with my wife, nigga before our kids lose one of their daddy's," Delante threatened.

"My bad, I mean no didn't mean no disrespect," Brian said, throwing his hands up in surrender position.

"Good because I don't want to have to kill your ass over my wife."

"On the phone you said you were just getting back in town?" I asked, changing the subject.

"Yea, I was down south for the last two weeks with my wife. Her mother was sick and eventually passed away. The kids didn't tell you?"

"No. In fact, Amira has been saying she was going over your house after school damn near every day," I told Brian. He looked at me with a puzzled look on his face. I yelled upstairs for Amira and Amir to bring their asses downstairs. I wasn't sure where the hell I went wrong with those two. They turned out to be everything I tried to prevent them from being. When they got down the steps, Amira's face was priceless.

"Amira, you father just informed me that he was away for damn near two weeks, so where the fuck where you going if you wasn't going to his house?" Amira started fidgeting with her fingers.

"So, is this when you was fucking? When you were supposed to be at your dad's?" I yelled.

"Whoa, what you mean, fucking? Amira, you're fucking. Since when?" Brian asked.

"That's not the half of it. Tell your dad that you whoever the little boy is had you walking around with Chlamydia and Trichomonas." Amira stood there crying and the room fell silent and I could literally see horns coming out of Brian's face.

"Who the fuck is this little boy? I should kill him and you," Brian snapped. For some reason, I watched my daughter cut her eye over at Kyree. I figured she was embarrassed, but something in my gut was telling me it was more than embarrassment. It was the look of fear.

"Kyree, I know you're not fucking my daughter," I blurted, causing the entire room to direct their attention to me and look at me like I was crazy.

"Ka 'Myra, you're out of pocket for that. Kyree is a grown ass man, not to mention that's her uncle. You need to chill, Ka 'Myra," Brain stated seriously.

"Then why is her uncle sweating bullets? Not to mention they have been cutting their eye at one another since she walked down the steps."

"I'm sorry, man. It only happened a few times," was the last thing Kyree said before he got rolled on by Brian, Delante, and Amir. The shit looked like something out of a movie. Meanwhile, my daughter was screaming at the top of her lungs.

I was in shock, and the only thing I knew was Kyree was gonna pay for this big time. He thought the ass whooping he was getting from them was something, I was about to ruin his entire life. If my kids weren't in the house, I would have shot that nigga with the gun that my husband thought I didn't know he had in the house.

"Please stop you're gonna kill him!" Amira hot ass yelled. It was so much blood flying everywhere and Kyree was pleading for his life. Finally, the whooping came to a stop when I heard Kamil and Kamar crying.

"Y'all go upstairs until I call you down. Go now," I yelled. The twins cried but did as I told them. I couldn't believe that Kyree of all people was fucking my daughter. I know that Amira had a body to die for, and she's a very pretty girl, but as a grown man and being the best friend of her father, he should have known better. But these men will fuck anything with a pussy.

"How could you fuck my daughter, Kyree? What type of sick pervert are you?" I yelled while kicking Kyree. He tried to move, but he couldn't. Kyree winced in pain like a little bitch. Even though Amira was a minor, I was very disappointed in her as well.

"Please stop I love him," Amira blurted. My eyes darted towards her with the death stare because I couldn't believe her dumb ass said some stupid shit like that.

"Do you know how fucking stupid you sound saying you're in love with a nigga that gave you two different std's? And not to mention, he's your dad's best friend. Do you really think he loves you, Amira? Let me answer that for you, he doesn't. You were just a fuck," I spat.

"You don't know what you're talking about. You swear you know every fucking thing, but you don't," Amira yelled. My heart fell to my stomach. I couldn't believe that my daughter was speaking to me like she lost her got damn mind. Oh, she was really feeling her damn self.

"Yo, Mira, you need to chill talking to mommy like that, especially over this pervert," Amir chimed in.

"There's nothing that any of you can do to keep me away from him. Baby, now that it's out, we don't have to sneak around anymore," Amira stated.

"Amira, I swear if you ever speak to me like that again, I will kill your dumb ass, and that's a promise. Y'all need to get this nigga out of my house before I shoot his ass," I threatened

I had so many different emotions running through my body at once, but the main one was hurt. I knew my daughter had been taken advantage of, and she didn't even realize it. But to disrespect me like I was a nobody over this nigga was a different kind of hurt. I didn't say another word, I just walked off to find Kamil and Kamar. I knew they had to be devastated at what they saw. I wasn't even sure how to explain what they witnessed. When I got to the twin's room, they were talking with Ms. Sara. I was glad that she came to their rescue. Ms. Sara was our live-in cook/nanny when needed.

"Thank you, Ms. Sara. I'll take it from here," I told her while walking in the room.

"Mommy, what's going on? Why were they beating up that man?" Kamil whined.

"Baby, let's not get into that. I'm sorry y'all had to witness that, but that man did something really bad. But you let us adults handle that. It will be dinner time soon, okay?"

"Okay. Mommy, can we come downstairs now? Maybe I can help daddy and Amir fight the bad man?" Kamar asked, causing me to chuckle. That boy was a mess. I guess they got that street side from their daddy. Although Delante wasn't in the streets anymore, the streets were definitely still in him, and I knew they always will be.

"Baby, they don't need any help and I didn't I say let the adults handle this. Just stay here. I'll be up to get y'all soon, I promise," I told them, kissing both of them on the cheek before heading back downstairs. When I got downstairs, Amir was picking up shit that fell during the fight, and Delante was pouring a drink. I didn't see Brian, Kyree or my disrespectful ass daughter of mine.

"Where the hell is everybody?" I asked.

"Daddy went to go dump that pedophile off at the hospital, and I don't know where Amira disappeared to," Amir answered. "I can't believe that Amira was messing with that nigga, what's wrong with your daughter?" Amir asked.

"I don't know, but I know if she ever talks to me like that again, it will be her last."

* * * * * *

A couple hours later, Amira's ass still wasn't home, and Brian said he still hasn't heard from her either, which meant she was probably at her best friend Latrice's house. After dinner, I would call Latrice's mom to find if she's there. And if so, her ass could stay there because I didn't feel like dealing with her shit tonight. I had to figure out how I wanted to handle Kyree's ass because there was no way in hell I was going to let him get away with that sick shit.

After dinner, as promised, I watched a movie with the kids but instead of popcorn, we had ice cream, candy and pretzels. Even Delante and Amir joined us. After Shark Tales went off, I gave the twins a bath and put them to bed. I called to confirm that Amira was at her best friend's house and that's where she was, so I let her hot ass be.

When I walked in my bedroom, Delante had candles lit and rose pedals laid out on the bed along with soft music playing. I didn't see him in the room so I went in the bathroom where I found him running bath water. Candles were lit in the bathroom as well. I looked over and he had a glass a wine in his hand.

"Delante, what's all this?" I asked.

"This is the start of me getting you relaxed and taking your mind off of all the bullshit that happened today. Then once we're done in here, I'm gonna take my wife into our bedroom, lay you on the bed and suck the soul out of pussy. Then I'm gonna make love to every inch of your body until the sun comes up in the morning." My pussy was instantly wet. I haven't had sex with Delante since I caught him getting his dick sucked, but I was well overdue. I wasn't gonna play hard to get tonight because I missed my husband.

After Delante was finished bathing me, he took me into our room and did everything he said he would do and more. Delante was trying to make a statement, and I read it loud and clear. The dick he was giving me was the best dick of my life. I couldn't believe that five years later, Delante still had new tricks up his sleeve and was still able to do the unimaginable to my body. After countless orgasms and a sore body, the sun was shining through the window, and I was just drifting off to sleep.

§*Chapter Eight*§

Tyisha

"Ahh shit! Calvin, don't stop. I'm about to cum, baby," I cooed as Calvin licked and sucked on my swollen clit.

"Come on, Ty, let me put this dick up in you?" Calvin pleaded. But his plea fell on death ears because I wasn't ready to cross that line with him just yet. Since I found out about Calvin cheating ways and him possibly having a baby on me, shit hasn't been the greatest between us. The one thing I was sure about was I knew I didn't want to be without my husband. I loved Calvin more than anything. But I still needed to take things slow and let him feel the pain a little longer. The only thing he could do for me right now is eat my pussy when I needed a nut. I still had needs and I was gonna have my needs met. He just wouldn't have the pleasure of penetrating me.

"Nah, I'm still not ready for all of that right now," I answered, getting up off the bed to clean myself up. Calvin was just gonna have to deal with the consequences of his actions.

My mother wasn't too happy with me for not divorcing Calvin, but that was my call and not hers. I didn't tell her how to run her marriage, and I didn't need her to tell me how to run mine. After taking a shower and getting dressed, I headed out the door. Today I was holding interviews for both of my boutiques. Both of my shops were doing well, and I could afford to hire more people for both shops since I had a lot more product and business. Plus, I really needed a manager because I wouldn't be in the boutiques as much anymore. I was focusing on being a mother and a wife while still making money.

Two hours later, I was finished doing my interviewing and decided on two new employees that stuck out to me more than the others did. Once I was done at work, I decided to be on my petty shit and go to the bank that bitch Nikki worked at. I told her getting me arrested was just the beginning of shit. That bitch had a lot of nerve calling the cops on me because she got her ass beat for fucking my husband. I walked into the bank looking like a million bucks, making sure to get in her line. When I was next in line, I smiled happily.

"Good afternoon, hoe. Just came to see if you fucked anybody else's husband this week?" I asked loudly so everyone could hear me. She just stood there looking retarded and call me petty if you want but I got a kick out of making her hoe ass uncomfortable.

"I didn't think your hoe ass would have anything to say. Anyway, enjoy the rest of your miserable day, hoe," I said before sashaying out of the bank.

"Hey, bestie. What's up? Did you hire anybody?" Ka 'Myra asked when I walked in her house.

"Hey, bestie. Yup, I hired four people. They gonna start Monday. You know next week is valentine's day week so people gonna be buying shit like crazy especially lingerie. But anyway, what's been going on over here?"

"Same shit. Amira is really smelling herself, and Kyree ass is still in the hospital for what I'm hearing. They fucked him up pretty bad. Outside of that not much, I'm gonna talk to Brittany's parents about throwing them a baby shower. Since she's having twins, she not expected to carry them full term. Delante and I have been doing pretty good. I think he's learned his lesson. I still haven't told him for sure that I was gonna remarry his black ass. I think I'll make him sweat until the day of. As a matter of fact, I'm gonna play a nice little trick on his ass. That'll teach his ass not to let another bitch suck his dick again," Ka 'Myra replied.

"Girl, you ain't shit, but I think it's a great idea. You know I'm in. I'm so sick of these niggas thinking they can do what they please and don't have to pay."

"Facts, so how are things between you and Calvin?"

"Girl, we're still rocky. I still haven't gave him no pussy, I just been making him eat it and keep it moving. He be mad as hell, but I don't care. I'll fuck him when I'm ready. And right now, I'm just not in that place," I told Ka'MyraKa'Myra honestly.

"I know the feeling. Sometimes I still feel like I don't want to forgive Delante, but I took wedding vows, and I love him, so I want us work. But I'm almost certain that if he was to ever cheat on me again in any kind of way, I would be done with him for good. I wouldn't be able to endure that type of pain again," Ka 'Myra stated.

"Yeah, I feel you on that, girl. And if I do stay, if it were to happen again, my ass will be cheating for sure. He would get a taste of his own medicine."

After talking to Ka 'Myra a little longer, it was time for me to pick up Cameron from school.

When I got home, I grabbed the mail, and my heart was racing when I saw the letter from DNA diagnostic center. Apart of me wanted to open it and read for myself, but instead, I called Calvin and told him it was here. I needed to see what was in my future. I wasn't sure that I would be able to stay with Calvin if that baby was his. If that little girl was his, that meant I would spend the rest of my life being reminded of my husband's affair, and that wasn't something my heart was set up to handle. I felt like if she wasn't his daughter, that would help us move past it quicker and we'll be able to move forward.

"Hey, baby. Wassup, you good?" Calvin answered.

"Yes, but where are you?"

"I'm actually on my way home. Are you sure that you're good?"

"The results just came and I'm ready to get this over with. These results determine our future," I told him honestly.

"Aight. I'll be there in about ten minutes," Cavin stated sadly. I guess he was just as scared as I was because he knew if that was his daughter that he would lose his family, and it would be his fault. I tried to find something to do for the next ten minutes, but I swear that it seemed like the longest ten minutes in the world. I finally heard the door open, and my heart started beating fast and hard against my chest. My fingers felt sweaty, I needed to pace myself quick. I was acting like I was about to find out one of my close relatives were dying. Calvin walked into the living room, and as usual, Cameron jumped up and ran over to Calvin as he did every day.

"Hey, son. Did you miss daddy?"

"Yes, I miss you every day, daddy! I think my mommy miss you too because when we came in the house, she starting being sad when she didn't see you," Cameron said, causing me to feel some type of way. We as parents never really realize how much of the shit we do affects our children.

"Well, daddy is home now, so it's no need for anyone to be sad, but I need you to go to your room so I can talk to mommy alone about some grown-up stuff."

"Daddy, did you do something bad again, and do we have to buy more stuff for mommy? Cameron asked with his hands up in the air.

"Nah, daddy is good. I haven't done anything bad. Now take your butt upstairs and stay out of grown folks business," Calvin answered. Cameron ran upstairs smiling.

"So, this is what you're teaching our son?" That when a man does something wrong, he has to buy something to make it better?"

"Well, it's the truth. I mean, it's more to it than that, but buying shit is a good start," Calvin replied. Niggas was crazy with their way of thinking.

"If you say so. Well, let's open this letter. I can't wait another second."

Calvin grabbed the envelope and ripped it open. I could have sworn I heard his heart beating. Calvin pulled the paper out of the envelope and read the results. Calvin rubbed his hands down his face.

"What does it say? Are you the father or not?" I asked anxiously. Calvin passed me the results and he wasn't the father. A sense of relief came over me yet I still found myself crying. Calvin wrapped his arms around me and held me tightly as I cried tears of relief.

"I'm so sorry, baby. I swear I'll never cheat on you again. I swear I will never cause you this much pain ever again in life," Calvin promised. I didn't know what to say, so I didn't say anything. I just laid there in his arms until the tears stopped.

****

The next morning when I woke up, I was feeling good, better than I have been feeling in the last few weeks. I got up and showered so I could get my day started. My mom was watching Cameron for me today while I do some running around with Ka 'Myra for this wedding in a few days. After getting me and Cameron dressed, I made him a quick breakfast then went into the office to make a few copies of some paperwork before heading out the door. After I dropped Cameron off, I had one more stop to make before meeting up with Ka 'Myra. I parked my car and walked over to Nikki's car and placed the DNA results on her window, then walked into the bank and passed out the results to some of the people that were at the bank. When I reached the windows, I gave her co-workers a copy as well. Then I passed her one.

"Everyone, if you're holding one of these papers and are unclear on what they are, these are this woman right here, DNA results. Not only did she sleep with my husband, she tried to pin her daughter on him, and as you all can see, it's not his fucking baby. Please beware of hoes like this," I yelled.

"Ma'am, you have to go. This is totally uncalled for," the security officer said, walking over to me.

"Don't worry I'm leaving and I have no reason to return. Bitch, if you ever contact my husband again, the ass-whooping, I'm gonna give you won't compare to the ass whooping I gave you before," I threw over my shoulder before walking out of the bank. I knew I was being beyond petty, but I didn't care. I was more pissed at her for having me arrested then I was for her sleeping with my husband. I blame that on him and he has had his share of embarrassment as well. I was the queen of petty, and I had no problem admitting it. Feeling like I accomplished my goal for the day, I headed to my Ka'MyraKa'Myra's house.

§*Chapter Nine*§

Delante

Shit has been super crazy. These last few weeks has been batshit crazy. Everybody had shit going on from the adults down to the damn kids that thought they were adults. Shit with me and Ka 'Myra has been going pretty good, but I still wasn't sure if she was gonna renew her vows on Valentine's Day. Deep down, I felt like she wasn't gonna leave me hanging, but I could never be too sure with Ka 'Myra. There was just some shit that she was not okay with, and this could very well be one of those things. I fucked up bad, letting that bitch suck my dick, but I'm glad I wasn't weak enough to fuck her. Otherwise, I was for sure I wouldn't have been a single man.

I just pulled up to Calvin's bike shop to what was up with him. He's been kinda of distant for the past few days and I wasn't sure why. When I walked in the shop, he was helping a customer out so I took it upon myself to go wait for him in his office. A few minutes later, Calvin walked in looking all sad and shit. I wasn't sure what the hell was going on with him.

"Yo, what's good? I been hitting you up and shit, and you been acting funny. You good?" I asked as soon as Calvin yellow ass walked in his office.

"Yea, I'm good. I've just been busy that's all," Calvin answered, and I knew it was more to what he said. I've known Calvin damn near my entire life, so I knew when something was wrong or that nigga was lying.

"Nigga, save that shit for somebody else. I'm your best friend for a reason, nigga now spill it. What the hell has you in your bag?"

"Honestly, I really think that I just need some pussy. All Tyisha do is let me eat it and that's it. She not fucking with a nigga right now. Then the other day I found out that the baby wasn't mine and shit and I can't lie, I'm a little upset that she isn't mine. But I have to sit around and act like I'm not bothered, so I don't have to hear no shit from Tyisha. I spent six months with that little girl. I'm the one that named her Kalie," Calvin vented.

"Damn, I can't even imagine, but look at it this way. You may have gotten attached, but at least you still have your family. I mean, nigga, you dodged a bullet. A big fucking bullet at that. You don't have to deal with girl Nikki either. You should be out celebrating, and as far as not getting no pussy, man up and take that shit. Her ass ain't gonna say no. I let Ka 'Myra ass off the hook for little but when I was ready to get my dick wet, I wined and dined that ass. Then told her I was about to make love to every inch of her body and that's what I did. And since that night, I've been in that pussy every night. I even been pulling out some new shit," I told him, and that nigga chuckled at my statement, but I was serious.

"Nigga, you're a fool, but I guess you're right about everything you said. But if I try that shit and she put me out, I'm coming to get some from your wife," Calvin joked. I didn't mind Calvin playing with me like that because I knew he would never cross that line. We both talk shit, but that's as far as it goes.

"Nigga, I ain't worried about you trying to fuck my wife unless you ready for your momma to wear that pretty black dress. Then once we bury your ass, I'ma fuck your wife and your momma," I threatened.

"Bitch, please. My wife or my mother wouldn't fuck your black ugly ass if I paid them to,' he shot back, causing me to laugh loud and hard. "Now, nigga, get the hell outta my office. I have work to do, but all jokes aside, thanks for checking up on. Plus, I needed that laugh."

"No problem. I gotta go anyway, but you got your tux and shit, right?"

"Yup, I'm ready," Calvin replied.

"Aight cool. Well, I'll holla at you later, nigga," I told Calvin before heading out.

When I got back home, I called for my pride and joys. It was Saturday afternoon and I took the day off from the studio so I could spend the day with my twins. Kamil talked me into taking them to the one place every kid loves, but every parent hates. Yup, I was about to take them to Chuck E. Cheese's.

"Kamil, Kamar, where are y'all?" I yelled upstairs. Kamil was the first one down the steps holding her favorite teddy bear.

"We right here, daddy. Is it time to go? I can't wait to play in the balls," she yelled. Kamar came down trying to be cool and shit wearing sunglasses. You had to love these kids. Kamil was still a baby at heart, but I knew deep down that we were gonna have some problems with Kamar. I could see me all through him, and for him to only be five, he talked like a ten year old sometimes older.

"Do we have to stay long, dad? That place is for babies," Kamar asked.

"It's not for babies. I'm not a baby and I want to go to Chuckie Cheese. Right, daddy, I'm not a baby?" Kamil whined.

"Yes, you are a baby," Kamar said.

"You do know we are twins, right? So if I'm a baby that you're baby too."

"Neither one of y'all are babies. Y'all are big kids, so cut it out, and Kamar, you know it's nothing wrong with Chuck E. Cheese's, so stop teasing your sister and let's go." Those two was about to drive me crazy with all that nagging about who's a baby and who's not, and they were both the same damn age.

§*Chapter Ten*§

Amira

"**M**ira, I been told you it was a bad idea to be fucking a grown ass man in the first place. He was just an older man, but he is literally older enough to be your daddy, not to mention he's your dad's best friend. What kinda sick pervert is he? Your dad's and brother had every right to beat his ass. Honestly, if that was my family, that nigga wouldn't even be breathing right now. So he made out good with a few broken bones. I don't know why you're so upset with your family. What the hell did you think they we're gonna do? And did you forget he burnt your hot ass?" My best friend, Latrice lectured. I mean, I knew she was probably right now, but I just wasn't in the mood to hear what she had to say right now.

Latrice and I have been best friends since we moved from the hood. She lived a couple blocks over, but we met in school and hit it off pretty quick. Even though she lived in Deptford, I could tell immediately that she was from the hood. My guess is this is where all the black hood folk moved to when they want to move from the hood. Latrice and I were the same age, but she grew up in the street life and my mom shielded us from that life as best as she could. But me and Amir always knew what was happening in the streets because we went to school in the hood, and the kids in the hood talked about everything that was going on. When me and Latrice first met, we hit it off immediately and been friends ever since. There was a lot of things that I did that my parents didn't know about, but I always played the good girl around them, and they brought it, so I ran with it.

My mom acts like she was gonna die when she found out about Amir fucking and having a baby, but I already knew how my brother was. We were actually one in the same. If she knew half the shit, we be doing, she would lose it. Amir knew shit about me but not everything because he was so overprotective, and to me, that was like having another parent. It's bad enough I already had two dads and a mom. Don't get me wrong; I loved having all that love from them. I couldn't ask for better parents. Half the time, I didn't know why I did the shit that I did.

"Latrice, I know, but I can't help that I fell for Kyree."

"Bitch, you didn't fall for no damn Kyree. You fell for that grown man dick, that's what you fell for," Latrice stated.

"Then how come I'm about to go visit him at the hospital?" I asked.

"Bitch, you better not. You must really want your parents to kill your hot ass; you need to chill. I don't think that's a good idea."

"I'll be quick, but I need to see him and make sure he's okay. Besides, I already ordered my Lyft. I'll be back before you know it," I told her. I was glad that my Lyft pulled up because I didn't feel like hearing her mouth.

Ten minutes later, I arrived at Cooper Hospital. When I walked in, I walked straight up to the receptionist's desk. I had to remember what the hell his last name was.

"Hi, may help you?"

"Yes, I'm here to see Kyree Williams," I stated, hoping that I had the right last name.

"May I ask what your relationship to the patient is?" I had to think fast.

"I'm his daughter," I lied. For some reason, that bitch snickered, and I didn't know what the fuck was so funny.

"You mind telling me what's so funny?"

"What's funny is that if you were his daughter, I'm sure his wife would have had you on the list. There's only one person that's on the list for visits, and that's his wife," she stated with a smug look on her face.

"My father isn't married?" I told her. I knew that bitch didn't know what she was talking about.

"Your father might not be married, but Kyree Williams is damn sure married," the receptionist said, laughing in my face.

"Look, little girl, you really need to go home before I call your father up here. I know who you are, Amira. Brian already informed me about my husband fucking you and giving you the same shit he gave me. Which is why my husband is laying up here with a broken rib cage now and a fractured face. I think you'll the last person my husband wants see."

I stood there speechless because I was in utter shock. How could I not know he was married? Then to just got played by his wife made me want to go hide under a rock and never show my face again. I didn't even bother to say another word; I just ran out the door in tears. I felt so stupid. He really did play me. He really was only using me for sex. I promise he was gonna pay for what he did to me. If it's the last thing I did, I was gonna get revenge.

I took my ass straight home and I was glad that when I got there no one was home. I wasn't sure where everyone was but I really didn't care. I went in my room and climbed into bed. I put the covers over my head and cried myself to sleep.

§*Chapter Eleven*§

Ka'Myra

Today was the big day. It was Valentine's Day and the day that I would renew my vows with Delante. In just one hour, I would be walking down the aisle for the first time. Although we were already married for some reason, this go around meant more to me than the first time. For one, we didn't have a wedding, and lastly, it meant that we were really in love. If you can spend five years with someone, go through ups and downs, and you're still willing to marry them for a second time, then the two of you are truly destined to be together. Some people can't make it a year, let a make it for five then do it again. I was in my dressing room with Tyisha, Amira, Kamil, and my stepmother, who just so happened to be my best friend's mother. I was giving my small wedding party their gifts, and my mother in law was making sure I had something old, something new, something borrowed, and something blue. I looked in the mirror and was very pleased with the way my hair and makeup looked. I was ready to cry, and I haven't even put on the dress yet.

Of course, Tyisha was my matron of honor, Amira was my maid of honor, and of course, Kamil was my flower girl. My bridal party looked beautiful. I decided to do a winter wonderland party since it was wintertime. The time arrived quickly for me to walk down the aisle, and the nerves in my stomach were doing backflips. I took one more look in the mirror and I looked simply beautiful. I looked and felt like a true Princess. Amira walked out first then Tyisha.

"Mommy, you said just slowly throw the flowers on the red carpet?" Kamil asked, breaking me from thoughts.

"Yes, baby, that's all you have to do. You throw them so I can walk on them when it's my turn to walk down," I told her.

"Well, who's gonna throw them down for me? I'm a princess too, so I want to walk on flowers like you," she said, causing me to laugh. This girl was something else.

"Just make sure you throw some down before you walk, so you'll get to walk on them too. Now go head. There waiting for us." Kamil did exactly what I said and she was perfect. From what I could see they landed perfectly in all the right spots.

The song "When I First Saw You," by Jamie Fox came on and everyone stood up to watch me come down the aisle. I was barely down the aisle before the waterworks started. I locked eyes with Delante and the nerves in my stomach subsided. That was just the type of effect Delante had on me. The only thing I could focus on was getting down the aisle and standing with my husband. My entire wedding party was looking good. My dad even cleaned up well. When we finally made it to the front, and my father gave me away to Delante, I was sure my makeup was ruined from all the crying I was doing. I was honored to have my dad give me away.

The ceremony went rather quick. It's funny how people spend thousands of dollars and months to a year to plan just to stand at the altar for ten short minutes. But for me, it was all worth it because I was now Mrs. Ka 'Myra Green for the second time, and it felt damn good. After taking a thousand pictures in my first dress, I changed into my second dress that was just as beautiful but just a lot more comfortable. The Valentine's day party had officially begun.

While everyone was on the dance floor partying, I was in my dressing room getting my pussy ate by my husband. After Delante made me climax twice, he bent my ass over and deep stroked me until we both came together. After we cleaned ourselves up, we went to join the party. We partied for hours before we went home and made love all night long until we both passed out. We woke up later on that afternoon and barely had time to wash our ass and get dressed because we had a flight to catch in two hours. But we made it work and caught our flight on time.

§*Chapter Twelve*§

Amira

Epilogue

(Six months later)

I wasn't sure what the hell had happened to Kyree because I never saw him again. It was kind of hard to get revenge on someone you didn't see or hear about. But it was cool, you live, and you learn. I actually had a boyfriend now, and my parents were okay with it since he was only two years older than me. His name was Ryan, and we worked together at the Footlocker in Deptford Mall. Although we had more money than we knew what to do with, my parents still raised us to work for our own shit and that I could appreciate. I was happy that me and my parents and finally moved past our issues because I hated not speaking to my parents like I used too. After the three of them sat me down and talked to me, I understood where they were coming from, and we've cool ever since. I vowed to do the right thing and to always be honest with them no matter what. Ryan was perfect; he wasn't a street dude, but he could handle himself. His parents also had money but made him work just like my parents made me work. We haven't had sex yet because I wanted to take things slow, but next week was his birthday, and I think that might be the night that it goes down.

Amir

I was now a proud father of twin girls and me and Brittany were still together. I could honestly say things weren't easy raising two kids at a young age. We had help and support from both sides of our family, but they still made us responsible for our own kids. We named our daughters, Brielle and Briana. Sometimes they were hard to tell apart; that's how much they looked alike. The only way you could tell them apart was from the birthmark that Briana had on the back of her neck. I loved my girls more than anything in this world. I went from not even wanting kids to not being able to live without them. Brittany's parents finally accepted me and we were pretty good. They told me they wished that had met the real me from the beginning instead of the good boy that wanted to be bad. I still wasn't as innocent as they thought I was; I just knew how to turn that shit down around them. Brittany was actually a great mother, and we were both still in school, and we still planned to go to college. So yeah, everything was going pretty well. I was glad that I had the type of mom that I did. My mom didn't play when it came to us, but she was only willing to accept our best and nothing less. I hope and pray that I do just half as good as she does for us, then I'll know I did a damn good being a father.

Calvin

I was finally over the fact that Kalie wasn't my daughter. Although in the beginning, it was a hard pill to swallow, I soon learned to count my blessings, I would have had Kalie, but I would of have lost Tyisha, as well as robbed my son the opportunity to be raised in a two parent household. I had to be the first to admit that we as adults never fully think of the damage that we cause to other people just because we deliberately choose to fuck up. I mean, not all things are deliberate, but fucking around on the person you're with is as deliberate as you can get. I mean, I don't know about any of you, but I have never accidently fell into some to some pussy.

Once I got the DNA results back stating that Kalie wasn't mine, it didn't take Tyisha long to move past it but she didn't have to worry about me cheating on her ass ever again. I learned my lesson the first time. Tyisha may have easily forgiven but it took my mother in-law up until a few months aga to let it go. I had to tell her ass off a few times, she was acting me and her were the ones married. The only reason I think she let it go when she did was because of Mr. Wilson. I guess he was just as tired of his wife as I was. I opened up another shop and that was going well so far. I have no complaints at the moment. My family was better than ever and my money flow was great. I couldn't ask for a better life.

Tyisha

I was so glad that shit worked out for the best with me and Calvin because I don't think we would have been here today if that baby would have turned out to be his. But I'm glad that he wasn't the father. Calvin and I were doing better than ever. Cameron was growing and patiently waiting for me to deliver his baby sister. Yup, you heard right. I was four months pregnant with a baby girl that I couldn't wait to spoil. After Calvin found out that the baby wasn't his, no matter how hard he tried to hide it, I knew my husband was disappointed. I just didn't say anything. He was entitled to feel how he wanted. But I figured why not just give him another baby, so I came off my birth control. Not much else has been going on besides me being a mother and a wife.

Oh yeah, my sex life is better than ever. I think I was still making up for when I put Calvin on Pussy punishment and stopped giving him some. Because my horny ass wanted dick all the time and my husband had no problem with delivering good dick on a daily basis.

Delante

I was on my way down to Atlantic City so I could sign my last bit of paper then I would officially be the new owner of ten casinos. I still kept my record label, but I didn't run it any longer. I was ready to try something new and see how much money this will bring in. I wasn't gonna have no regular casino that was too easy. I was adding some extra shit. My hotels were gonna be like some shit you could only dream about but for a low rate. Married life was great. I couldn't ask for a better family. I was a Pop-Pop and I was in love with Brielle and Briana. I honestly wanted at least one more baby with Ka'MyraKa'Myra, but she wasn't having it. She told me there was no way she was willing to risk popping out two more babies. Plus, she didn't want to raise kids with our grandkids. I didn't mind having more, I just didn't want any more girls. Especially after that shit that went down with Amira and that bitch ass nigga Kyree. God rest his soul; there was no way in hell I was letting that nigga breathe after what he did.

I mean, his death is still a mystery to everyone. I didn't even tell Ka'MyraKa'Myra what had done. I had a couple connects at the hospital, so I used it to my advantage. I paid her two hundred and fifty thousand dollars to shoot that dumb ass nigga with some deadly shit that I made up, but it worked, and that nigga was no longer breathing. I just hope and pray that another nigga don't try me again when it comes to mine. I may not have been Amir and Amira's biological father, but they were still mine.

Ka'Myra

"Push! I can almost see the head, just relax," I told my patient Tiara. Even though I still had my shops and did hair from time to time, I was now focused on my new business. I decided to open up a group home for single young parents. You could be a single mother or father, we supplied their every need. The only thing the parents had to do was job training and attend a parent group session twice a month, and that was it.

We made sure to have a labor and delivery doctor in the faciality for the woman that was pregnant. We accepted children from the ages of thirteen to the age of twenty we gave them one year to get on their feet with our assistance. We even had a childcare on the premise. I loved doing this even though I wasn't getting paid for it I didn't care I just wished someone would have helped me when I was in these parents shoes. Right now I have three teen girls and two teen boys. The house can fit up to ten families. I'm just getting it off the ground. Tyisha said she would come help out after she had the baby. As far as my home life, everything was going great. I was enjoying my granddaughters; they were the cutest little things. My husband was enjoying them a little too much because he was constantly talking about me having another baby, and that shit wasn't happening. I was done with having kids. And even if I would have considered having one more, which I'm not, I can't get past the thought of having another set of twins.

I was proud of Amir for stepping up and doing what he needed to do for his family. I was also proud of the changes Amira made because I was about to kill her hot ass when I found out about her fucking Kyree's ass. I'm not sure what the hell happened to him, but I was almost sure that my husband was behind it. I didn't care as long as he kept his ass away from my daughter. I was feeling like I did something right when it came to my kids. I wasn't nowhere near done raising kids. I still had a five year old set of twins running around. Kamil still was my baby, but Kamar seemed to grow up on me a little faster than I thought he would. I mean, he wasn't grown or disrespectful, he just acted a little older than what he was.

Overall, life was good. I couldn't have asked for a better life. I may have started off with a block boy, but I ended up with my cupid, my knight in shining armor, my heartbeat, and the air that I breathe. Five years later, we're still going strong, and I know in my heart that we'll be going for a lifetime more.

The End!

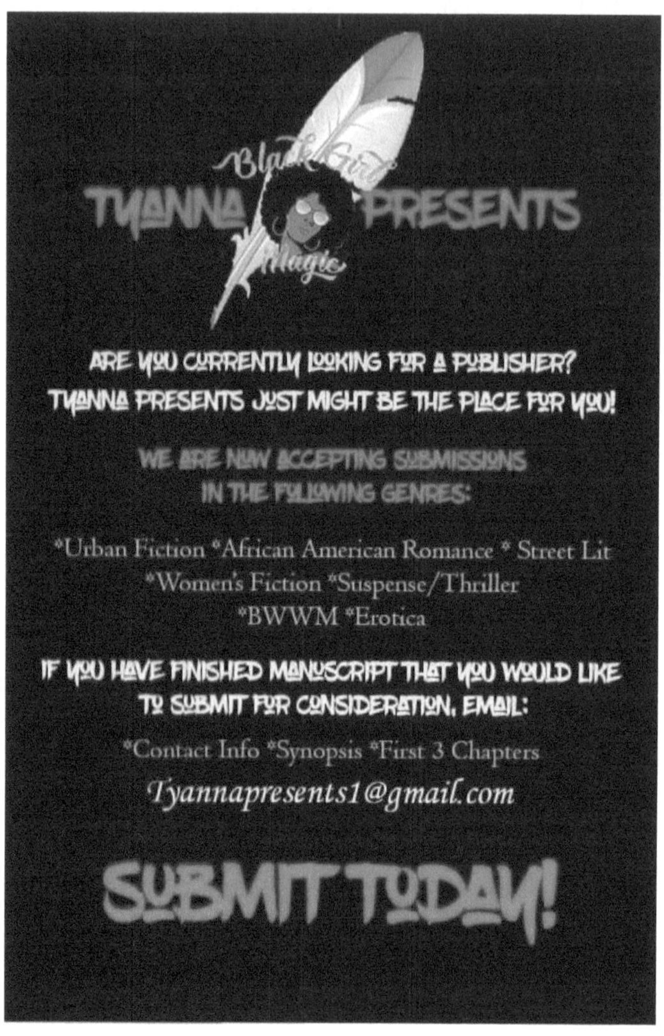
TYANNA PRESENTS

ARE YOU CURRENTLY LOOKING FOR A PUBLISHER?
TYANNA PRESENTS JUST MIGHT BE THE PLACE FOR YOU!

WE ARE NOW ACCEPTING SUBMISSIONS
IN THE FOLLOWING GENRES:

*Urban Fiction *African American Romance * Street Lit
*Women's Fiction *Suspense/Thriller
*BWWM *Erotica

IF YOU HAVE FINISHED MANUSCRIPT THAT YOU WOULD LIKE
TO SUBMIT FOR CONSIDERATION, EMAIL:

*Contact Info *Synopsis *First 3 Chapters
Tyannapresents1@gmail.com

SUBMIT TODAY!